Walt Disney's

Donald Duck and the Big Dog

Originally published as *Donald Duck and the Biggest Dog in Town*

A GOLDEN BOOK • NEW YORK
Western Publishing Company, Inc., Racine, Wisconsin 53404

 Library of Congress Catalog Card Number: 85-81573
ISBN 0-307-02077-0
F G H I J

"Uncle Donald!" cried Huey, Dewey, and Louie. "Guess where we're going!"

"No one's going *anywhere* without breakfast," said Donald Duck.

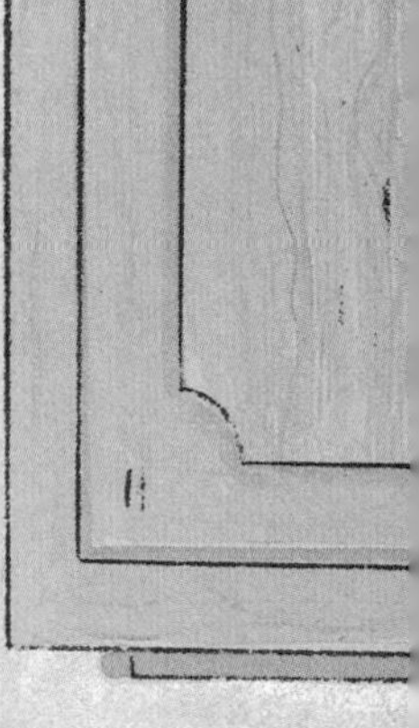

"We don't mean *today,*" said Huey. "There's going to be a dog show. The dog who does the most tricks wins."

"First prize is a trip to Hawaii," said Dewey.

"And *we're* going to win!" said Louie.

"That's going to be pretty hard," said Donald. "You don't have a dog."

"We'll get one at the animal shelter," said Huey. "Those dogs need good homes."

"No dogs in this house!" warned Donald. "They get fur all over the place and have to be walked and fed."

"We'll brush it and feed it and walk it," said Louie.

"They climb on the furniture," said Donald.

"We'll build a doghouse," said Dewey.

"Oh, all right," Donald said finally.

As soon as they finished breakfast, Huey, Dewey, and Louie went with Donald to the animal shelter.

"We'd like to get a dog," Donald said to the man at the desk. "A nice *small* dog."

"I have a nice dog named Ragmop," said the man. "But he's not small."

"How big is he?" asked Donald.

"Wait here," said the man. "I'll show you."

HORIZED
ONNEL
LY

In a minute, the man was back with Ragmop.

"He's great!" shouted Huey, Dewey, and Louie. "We'll take him!"

"Just a minute," squawked Donald. "He's the biggest dog in town!"

"*Please,* Uncle Donald," begged his nephews.

Ragmop wagged his tail and licked Donald's hand.

"He likes you, sir," said the man.

"Okay," sighed Donald. "We'll take him."

As soon as they got outside, Ragmop bounded ahead.

"Don't let go of his leash!" yelled Donald.

The big dog galloped happily down the street, with Donald and his nephews scrambling behind.

When they got home, Donald stumbled inside to take a nap.

"Come on," said Dewey. "Let's build the doghouse."

The boys got a hammer and some boards and nails and started to work. A few hours later, Donald came outside.

"We're ready to paint now!" Louie told Donald. He opened a large can of yellow paint, and carefully put the lid on the grass.

Ragmop trotted over and stepped right on top of the paint-covered lid.

"I'll bet we have the only dog around town with a yellow paw!" Louie said with a laugh.

The next morning, Huey, Dewey, and Louie began to teach Ragmop some tricks. He learned to wave one paw...flap his ears...and stand on his front legs.

“Ragmop’s terrific,” said Louie. “Soon he’ll be doing lots more tricks.”

“He’s not bad, not bad at all,” said Donald. “Maybe we really will get to Hawaii.”

In the afternoon, Daisy stopped by to see Ragmop's new tricks. As she came around to the back yard, she noticed a strange man peeking through the fence.

"Who is the man with the red sweater?" she asked Donald and the boys.

Huey ran over to look. But by the time he got to the fence, the man was gone.

"I wonder who he was," said Huey.

The next morning, the man was back.

"He was peeking through the fence again," said Dewey. "When I asked who he was, he ran away."

"Look," said Louie. "He got his sweater caught on a branch."

Two days later, they found huge footprints in the mud.

"I'll bet they belong to that man who was watching us the other day," said Dewey. "I wonder why he keeps coming back."

"It's sort of scary," said Louie. "I hope nothing else happens."

But something else did happen. The next day was the dog show, and Ragmop was gone! "I hope no one's taken him!" said Huey.

Donald, Daisy, and the boys looked all over town, but Ragmop was nowhere to be found.

Then they passed the dog show, and they heard the crowd cheering and clapping.

"Let's look over there," said Daisy. "Maybe Ragmop saw some other dogs on their way to the show, and followed them."

The winning dog was waving to the crowd.

"His owner has awfully big feet!" said Huey.

"And his red sweater is torn!" said Dewey.

"Just like the man who was peeking through our fence!" said Louie.

"But that dog doesn't look like Ragmop," said Daisy.

The dog turned and waved to Donald and the boys. Suddenly Donald's eyes went wide. He ran up to the judge.

"That dog is ours!" he squawked. "Ragmop stepped in yellow paint the other day, and some of it is still on his paw!"

The man's face turned as red as his sweater. "Ragmop was so good at tricks," he said, "I knew he'd win the trip to Hawaii. So I took him home and gave him a haircut. I didn't think anybody would recognize him!"

"It looks like you folks are the winners," the judge said as he gave Donald plane tickets for everyone.

Daisy hugged Ragmop. "Don't worry," she said. "Your fur will grow back soon. Besides, when you see how hot Hawaii is, you'll be glad you had a haircut!"